THE TALE OF A PIG

A Caucasian Folktale

THE

TALE

OF A

PIG

Adapted and Illustrated by Wallace Tripp

McGRAW-HILL BOOK COMPANY
New York • Toronto • London • Sydney

To Marcy

Library of Congress Catalog Card Number: 68-13103

1234567890 HDEC 7543210698

There was once an old woodsman who lived with his wife in a little cottage at the edge of a great forest. Although they had no children, they were not quite alone, for living with them was a most unusual creature—a rather small, a rather pink, a rather clever pig.

Just how clever she was, you shall see.

Bright and early she would arise and sweep the steps.
Then she would go to the bin, get the grain, and feed the
chickens.

After that she would gather twigs for the fire and bake
the most delicious dark bread. While it was baking on
the hearth, she would take a straw basket and jig-jog
into the forest to gather berries.

One day as she picked berries in a glade deep in the woods, she was spied by a rider on a great dappled horse. He marveled to see her plucking the red berries from the high bushes, and he was even more surprised at how gently she placed them in the basket.

8

But his eyes nearly popped from his head when the pig stepped into the dancing sunlight, turned thrice about, and changed into a beautiful young maiden.

In clear, sad tones she sang:

> By a marriage token
> This spell will be broken;
> Till a man I marry,
> As a pig I'll tarry.

11

It so happens that the rider who watched her was very much a man, and a prince to boot.

The maiden danced gaily in the glade, but too soon the dainty hands became hard little hoofs, the slender neck became short and stout, and she was a pig once more. She plodded home with her berries, followed, as you might imagine, by the Prince.

After the pig had gone inside the cottage, the Prince sprang from his horse and rapped on the woodsman's door.

"Good morning, sir," said the Prince to the old man.

"Welcome, my lord," replied the woodsman. "Won't you come in for a glass of ale and a bowl of berries?"

"We can offer no more," said the woodsman's wife, "but I assure you the ale is old, and the berries are the freshest to be had."

The Prince gladly accepted.

After some pleasant conversation, he asked the old couple if they would sell the pig.

"Oh, no," replied the woodsman's wife. "We cannot sell her. She sews, she bakes, she washes. And we are old and tired and poor. We could not survive without her."

The Prince placed upon the table a fair-sized leather

sack filled with gold. "Would this change your mind?"

The woodsman and his wife hesitated.

"And a new sack each time the old one empties," the Prince added.

The couple could not refuse, for now they could afford all the servants they would ever need, to say nothing of cellars full of ale and whole forests full of berries.

So the Prince took the pig and rode to his father's castle.

"Father," he said to the King, "I wish to marry this little pig."

The King stared in disbelief. Then he began to turn red, and then purple. He roared, he raged, he bellowed. He stomped, he pounded, he shook. And for two hours by the castle clock, he fumed and carried on.

At last he yelled, "Guards, lock the Prince up! He has gone mad!" Then he sank exhausted onto his throne.

For two weeks the Prince brooded in his cell. At last the King appeared, carrying a large key. "Do you still wish to marry this pig?" he inquired.

"Yes," the Prince replied firmly, "I do."

"Well, then," sighed the King, "if you must." And he unlocked the Prince's cell. "Your brains have clearly turned to pudding anyway."

And so the wedding took place.

The guests were at first astonished by the unusual spectacle before them, but soon their amazement turned to amusement at seeing the handsome, smiling Prince standing beside the plump little bride. As for the King, he merely hung his head and muttered to himself.

21

At the end of the ceremony, the Prince knelt and said softly:

> By this marriage token
> The spell is now broken.

And once more, for the last time, the little pig changed into the beautiful maiden. The guests, who had before snickered with amusement, now gasped with wonderment and admiration. The poor King now began to think his own brains were turning to pudding. But he was so overjoyed, he did a little dance and drank numerous toasts to the health of the future king and queen.

But, like a pig's tail, our tale takes an unusual turn.

The King's Captain of the Guard, in some ways a curious fellow, had watched enviously as the pig changed into a maiden.

For days after the wedding, he pondered what he had seen. He would mutter and snort and scratch his head.

24

"Why," he would say in his arrogant way, "if I were to seek out the biggest, fattest pig in the kingdom, would it not, if I were to marry it, turn into the most beautiful maiden in all the land?"

Reasoning thus, he saddled his horse.

He filled his saddle bags, and traveled across the kingdom, up hill, down dale, and by numerous sites, in search of the pig of his dreams.

Many weeks had passed when the tired Captain rode into a rickety, run-down farm. A slovenly farmer appeared and grumbled, "What do you want?"

"Some food and drink, if you have it, and a look at your pigs, if you have any," the Captain answered.

"We have no food or drink. Not for you, anyhow," the farmer replied. "But the pigs are out back if you want to look."

In a wretched, dirty sty filled with mud lolled a number of particularly fat, ugly pigs. Soon the biggest pig the Captain had ever seen reared itself like a mountain from the muck. The Captain knew his search was ended.

After paying an enormous sum, the Captain waded
into the sty to pull the beast out. It ran wildly about,
and the Captain went splashing after it.

When he had caught it, he tried to lift the pig onto his horse, but alas, it was far too big. The poor Captain had to hire the farmer's cart to haul the squealing sow back to the castle.

Days later the bedraggled Captain plodded through the castle gate with his bride-to-be.

The wedding was a catastrophe. The pig ran about, bit ladies, tipped over chairs, snorted and squealed, dashed and crashed.

The confused ceremony at last over, the Captain shouted above the pig's squeals, "Now for goodness' sake, change into a beautiful maiden!" He knelt and said:

By this marriage token
The spell is now...

And with that, the pig kicked the Captain and
thundered through the castle and out the gate, never
to be seen again.